Whistler's Last Song

Written by Adam Herro
Illustrated by Mark Doublin

The common childhood misconceptions about death and dying voiced by the characters in this story are further detailed and discussed in the collection of grief research entitled *Children Mourning Mourning Children* edited by Kenneth J. Doka, Ph.D. (Hospice Foundation of America, 1995).

ISBN 978-1-61225-192-9

Published by Mirror Publishing
Milwaukee, WI 53214

Printed in the USA.

This book is dedicated to _____.
You are loved.
Always and forever.

Nestled deep in the woods, amongst one of the tallest trees, lived the Leaf family. There was Papa Oak, Mama Maple, and their two children Leafy and Whistler.

Whistler is the youngest in the family and was born with a hole in his tummy. Every night when the winds blew across his belly, his tummy would whistle a beautiful melody for the whole forest to hear.

All the animals of the forest knew and loved Whistler. They were all Whistler's friends. His song put the sheep and foxes to sleep side by side and made the coyotes sing in harmony. Whistler brought peace to the forest's night.

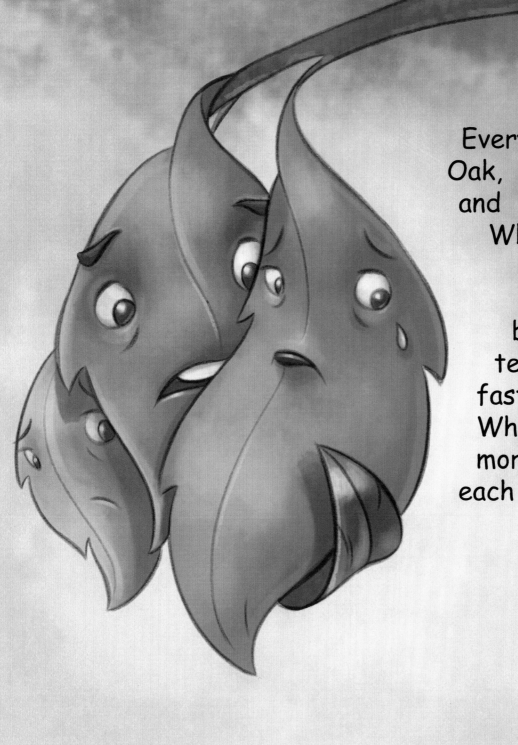

Every time Papa Oak, Mama Maple, and Leafy heard Whistler's soft melody, they would cry bittersweet tears, for the fast winds bent Whistler's stem more and more each night.

Without a full and healthy body, Whistler cannot protect his young stem from breaking away from the tree. Without the life support from the tree, Whistler would die.

After a night of strong winds throughout the forest, the Leaf family realized it was time to say good-bye to Whistler. Tonight, Whistler will perform his last song for the entire forest to hear.

Whistler spent his last day with his family. Together, they bathed in the sweet morning dew and felt the rays of sun on their bodies.

Some birds even stopped by and arranged branches to help support Whistler's weak stem. It was a special day for Whistler and his family.

As the night approached, Leafy turned to her Mama and Papa. "I am going to miss Whistler so much. I don't understand why he has to die." As Papa Oak and Mama Maple leaned in to hug Leafy, the Leaf family saw all the animals of the forest gathered below their tree.

Like Leafy, the animals had some questions about death, too. Papa Oak was old and wise and had seen many leaves blossom and fall throughout his life. The animals knew he would be able to help them understand.

Suddenly, the bear spoke. "Do you know when I will die Papa Oak?"

Papa Oak responded: "No one knows for sure when you or anyone will die, Mr. Bear. All we know is that at some point every one of us will die. That's why we must be thankful for everyday just like Whistler."

"Not me," said the Fox. "I'm cunning and tricky. I'll fool death and escape!"

"I'm sorry," Papa Oak said. "Death will even come to you Fox no matter how smart you are because death is not some animal or person that can be tricked or fooled. Just as the sun rises and sets or the spring turns to winter, every life experiences a beginning and an end."

Then the Owl cooed: "Papa Oak, I think Whistler is dying because of me. A couple weeks ago I wished he would stop whistling at night so I could hoot and whoo for the whole forest to hear.

I wished it and now it's coming true. I am so sorry."

"It is not your fault Owl," said Papa Oak. "Our sweet Whistler is dying because of the hole in his tummy, not because of your wishes. Leaves, animals, and even people do not die because of wishes or thoughts. They die because something important is not working inside their bodies anymore."

After wiping her tears, Leafy spoke to Papa Oak. "When Whistler falls from the tree, will he grow back again?"

"Well," Papa Oak said. "Once Whistler breaks from his stem he will die and never be able to return. New leaves will be born, but none will have the heart of Whistler."

"But where will Whistler's spirit go?" howled the coyote.

To which Papa Oak said: "Whistler's spirit will stay here in the forest with all of us and we will never forget the peace he brought us."

As night fell, the winds blew harder and harder. All the animals stayed around the tree to express their love to Whistler and his family. Papa Oak, Mama Maple, and Leafy tried their best to support Whistler against the harsh winds, but the hole in his tummy left him weak.

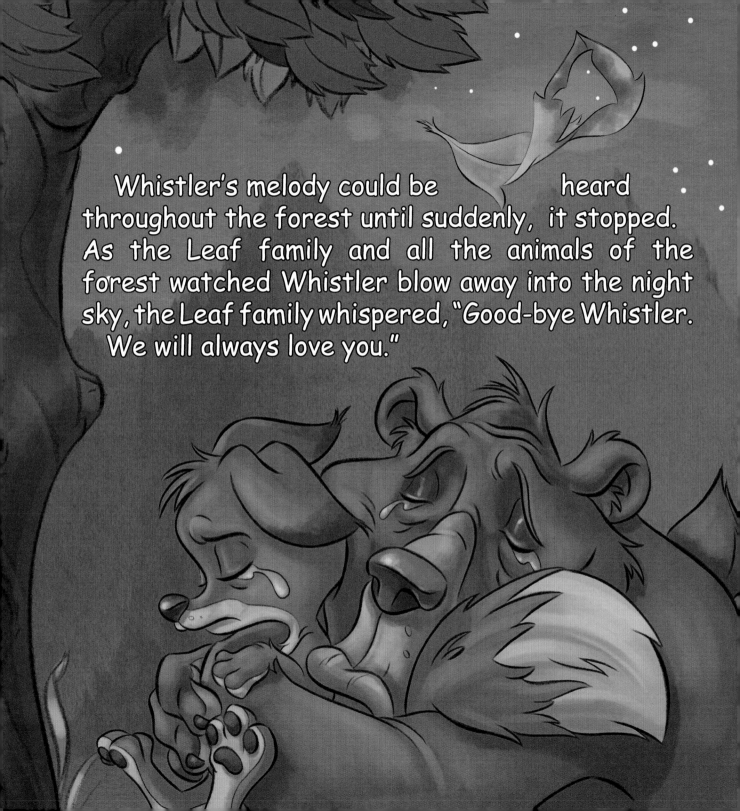

Whistler's melody could be heard throughout the forest until suddenly, it stopped. As the Leaf family and all the animals of the forest watched Whistler blow away into the night sky, the Leaf family whispered, "Good-bye Whistler. We will always love you."

To honor Whistler with the peace he so often brought all his friends in the forest, the animals sung with all the love in their hearts so their cries could be heard throughout the forest.

As Papa Oak, Mama Maple, and Leafy listened to the animals' song, Leafy turned to Mama Maple and said, "Why did Whistler have to die?"

Mama Maple thought for a moment and then spoke. "No one really knows why Whistler or anyone has to die. We only have our beliefs. I believe Whistler's death reminds our family and all the animals of the forest how special life is. Every time we think of Whistler we will remember how lucky we are to have met him. And every time I think of you Leafy, I will remember how lucky I am to still share a branch with you."

The next night the forest was silent, but if the Leaf family and the animals listened closely to their hearts, the memory of Whistler's peaceful melody could still be heard.